H KAUR

Friendship, Family and Fireworks

Copyright © 2024 by H Kaur

All rights reserved. No part of this publication may be reproduced, stored or transmitted in any form or by any means, electronic, mechanical, photocopying, recording, scanning, or otherwise without written permission from the publisher. It is illegal to copy this book, post it to a website, or distribute it by any other means without permission.

This novel is entirely a work of fiction. The names, characters and incidents portrayed in it are the work of the author's imagination. Any resemblance to actual persons, living or dead, events or localities is entirely coincidental.

H Kaur asserts the moral right to be identified as the author of this work.

H Kaur has no responsibility for the persistence or accuracy of URLs for external or third-party Internet Websites referred to in this publication and does not guarantee that any content on such Websites is, or will remain, accurate or appropriate.

Designations used by companies to distinguish their products are often claimed as trademarks. All brand names and product names used in this book and on its cover are trade names, service marks, trademarks and registered trademarks of their respective owners. The publishers and the book are not associated with any product or vendor mentioned in this book. None of the companies referenced within the book have endorsed the book.

First edition

This book was professionally typeset on Reedsy. Find out more at reedsy.com

Contents

Chapter 1: Introducing Simran	1
Chapter 2: Laura's World	5
Chapter 3: The Shopping Trip	7
Chapter 4: Family Ties	11
Chapter 5: Roots and Resilience	15
Chapter 6: The Wisdom of Dadi	19
Chapter 7: Rajinder's Balancing Act	21
Chapter 8: Disco Preparations and Unbreakable Bonds	23
Chapter 9: The Night Comes Alive	28
Chapter 10: Morning Reflections and Family Threads	33
Chapter 11: The Calm Before the Storm	38
Chapter 12: Shadows of Crisis	43
Chapter 13: Facing Traditions	49
Chapter 14: A Celebration to Remember	55

Chapter 1: Introducing Simran

The faint hum of Bhangra music echoed from the kitchen as Simran Gill perched on the window ledge of her room, gazing down at the bustling street of Southall. The rich aroma of turmeric and cumin from her mother's cooking seeped into every corner of their semi-detached house, mingling with the earthy smell of rain from the open window. Outside, her siblings darted in and out of the garden, their laughter blending with the distant sound of the fruit vendor's cart.

Simran, 15 years old and brimming with ideas and opinions, was the eldest of the Gill siblings. She had a knack for balancing her role as a responsible older sister and a fun, carefree teenager. Her younger sisters, Preeti and Amrita, idolised her, often copying her hairstyles or asking for her advice on school projects. Her little brother, Manveer, was an energetic whirlwind who lived to annoy her, but his cheeky grin always melted her frustration.

Their family home was a lively haven, filled with children's chatter, the rhythmic clacking of her mum's sewing machine, and her father's occasional booming laugh when his favourite cricket team scored a six.

Simran glanced at her desk, cluttered with textbooks, her prized Disc-man, and a stack of freshly burned RnB mix CDs from Zara. The 1990s had brought its own flavour to life – from baggy jeans and chokers to Nokia phones and dial-up internet. Yet, among all the cultural shifts, Southall remained its own world, a vibrant hub of Punjabi life in London. The local gurdwara stood as a cornerstone of their community alongside the bustling Broadway Market and its rows of saree shops, sweet marts, and gold jewellers.

Simran often walked these streets with her best friends, Laura, Kiran, and Zara. They were an eclectic group. Kiran, who was as calm and steady as a monsoon drizzle, had been her friend since childhood. Zara, with her daring red lipstick and infectious confidence, was the trendsetter of the group. And then there was Laura – Simran's best friend – a whirlwind of wit and sarcasm who came from a completely different world.

Laura's life couldn't have been more different from Simran's. She lived in a cramped council flat with peeling wallpaper, surrounded by the chaos of her four older sisters. Two of them had left home under complicated circumstances, leaving Laura in the thick of a messy, volatile environment. Her parents' fights often filled the flat, their voices carrying through the thin walls. But Laura, sharp and determined, had carved her own path. She envied the stability of Simran's home, where there was always a plate of warm roti waiting for her and a quiet corner to escape to when her own house felt too loud.

Simran's mum, Baljeet, treated Laura as one of her own. A petite woman with a quick smile and nimble hands, Baljeet spent her days sewing clothes for big-name stores like Topshop

Chapter 1: Introducing Simran

and Marks & Spencer. The work was exhausting, but it kept the household afloat. Baljeet's laugh was soft and warm, but her resilience was unyielding. Simran often marvelled at how her mum balanced so much with so little complaint.

Downstairs, Simran heard her mum call out, "Simran, help Preeti with her math homework before she starts crying again!"

"Coming, Mum!" Simran shouted back, rolling her eyes with a smile. She stretched her arms and stood up, her reflection catching her attention in the mirror. With her jet-black hair in a loose ponytail and a sprinkle of freckles across her nose, she thought she looked just fine for a girl who had barely survived the jungle that was Year 10.

As she descended the stairs, she heard her dad chatting loudly on the phone. Rajinder Gill, her father, was the glue of the family – a pleasant man who worked long hours as a minicab driver but always made time for his children. He had a cheeky sense of humour and a soft spot for his mother, Simran's dadi.

Dadi, or Grandma as her non-Punjabi friends called her, was a character all on her own. Fiercely traditional, she had a sharp tongue and was often critical of Baljeet. Yet Simran had overheard her on multiple occasions praising her mum to her friends, calling her the "best daughter-in-law" anyone could ask for. Baljeet, for her part, treated Dadi with unwavering kindness, laughing off her jibes with a grace that left Simran in awe.

"Simran, beta," her dad said, covering the phone with his hand. "Your dadi's coming over tonight, so don't leave your shoes all over the hallway, haan?"

Simran nodded, already anticipating the lively evening ahead. Whenever Dadi visited, the house became a hub of activity, with endless chai and gossip flowing even faster.

Friendship, Family and Fireworks

As the family gathered around the table for dinner that evening, the conversation turned to the upcoming school disco.

"Men in Black outfits, huh?" her dad teased when Simran mentioned her plans. "Very clever. But remember, beta, no funny business."

Simran laughed, promising to keep things PG. But her mind was already racing with excitement—the shopping trip to Bluewater, the party, the music, and the sheer thrill of being 15 in the 1990s.

Chapter 2: Laura's World

Laura Mason slammed the front door of her flat shut and leaned against it, exhaling a long breath. Inside, the smell of stale cigarette smoke clung to the air like an unwanted guest. Her dad was slouched on the sofa, watching TV with a can of lager balanced precariously on the armrest. Her mum was nowhere to be seen, probably out running errands or visiting her sister.

The living room was a mess! Empty crisp packets, newspapers, and mismatched socks scattered across the carpet. It was a far cry from the tidy, lively home she loved visiting at Simran's house. Laura's flat always felt heavy, like the weight of everyone's problems had soaked into the walls.

"Oi, Laura, grab me another one from the fridge," her dad called without looking away from the screen.

Laura ignored him and hurried to her bedroom, slamming the door shut behind her. She flopped onto her unmade bed, staring up at the cracks in the ceiling. She loved her family, of course, but sometimes it felt like she didn't belong here.

Her sisters had left a trail of chaos in their wake. Amanda,

Friendship, Family and Fireworks

the eldest, moved out after falling pregnant at 17, and Sarah followed suit a year later. The two middle sisters, Chloe and Diane, were still living at home but rarely spoke to Laura unless it was to argue. The only place Laura felt truly understood was Simran's house.

Simran's mum, Baljeet, treated Laura like one of her own. When Laura stayed over for dinner, Baljeet would pile her plate high with saag and makki di roti, always adding, "Have more, beta," until Laura couldn't eat another bite. And Kiran's mum was no different. The two women had taken Laura under their wing, much to the disapproval of their gossipy friends.

"They're good girls," Kiran's mum would say whenever someone raised an eyebrow at Laura's family. "Respectful and hardworking. That's what matters."

Laura was grateful for them, but a part of her always felt out of place when she saw the warmth and stability in Simran's home. It wasn't jealousy, exactly—more like longing.

Her phone buzzed, snapping her out of her thoughts. A text from Simran flashed on the screen:

Simran: "Bluewater tomorrow! Can't wait. What time can you meet me?"

Laura smiled for the first time that day. Shopping with Simran was like a mini-vacation. The chaos of her home life disappeared, replaced by laughter, inside jokes, and the thrill of trying on outfits they could never afford.

Laura: "1 pm. Bus stop near the library. Can't wait!"

The promise of the trip lifted her spirits. She could already picture herself in a sleek Men in Black blazer, impressing Nick Patel at the disco.

Chapter 3: The Shopping Trip

The next day, Simran stood at the bus stop near the library, her breath curling in the crisp November air. She hugged her denim jacket tighter and glanced at her watch. Laura was running late, as usual.

A double-decker bus roared past, splashing a puddle near Simran's feet. She stepped back just in time, muttering, "Typical Southall weather."

"Oi, you're early for once!" Laura's voice rang out. She came jogging toward Simran, her long coat flapping behind her. Her cheeks were flushed from the cold, and her messy ponytail made her look like she'd just rolled out of bed.

"I said one o'clock," Simran teased. "You're lucky I'm patient."

Laura grinned, hooking her arm through Simran's. "C'mon, let's go. Bluewater waits for no one!"

The bus ride to Kent was anything but boring. The two girls snagged seats at the top deck and began planning their shopping spree immediately.

"We'll start with the fancy dress shops," Simran said, pulling

Friendship, Family and Fireworks

out a list she'd scribbled on a scrap of paper. "Then shoes, then lunch. Oh, and we *have* to hit Our Price. I need that new RnB compilation CD Zara was talking about."

Laura nodded, her eyes sparkling. "And don't forget the gadget shops. I've been saving up for one of those Tamagotchis."

They chatted nonstop, laughing at their own jokes and swapping stories about their other friends. Simran told Laura about Zara's latest dramatic makeover—a daring fringe that had the whole school talking—and Laura shared how Kiran had been roped into helping her mum organise a community event at the gurdwara.

The bus slowed as Bluewater Shopping Centre loomed into view. Its glassy façade gleamed even in the dull afternoon light.

"Whoa," Laura breathed. "I forgot how massive this place is."

Simran grinned. "Welcome to paradise."

Inside, the girls were hit with a wave of warm air and the mingling scents of fresh pretzels and department store perfumes. They darted into the first clothing shop they saw, rifling through racks of blazers and trousers.

"Men in Black, right?" Laura held up a pair of sleek black pinstriped trousers. "These are perfect."

Simran grabbed a matching blazer from another rack. "Try them on! I'll find shoes while you change."

Laura disappeared into the fitting room while Simran browsed the footwear section. She found a pair of glossy black loafers and held them up triumphantly. When Laura emerged, Simran let out a low whistle.

"You look amazing!" she said, spinning Laura around. The trousers fit perfectly, and the blazer gave her an effortlessly cool vibe.

"Your turn," Laura said, shoving Simran into a fitting room

Chapter 3: The Shopping Trip

with her own set of clothes.

Simran slipped into the outfit and examined herself in the mirror. The sharp lines of the blazer and trousers gave her a polished look, but it was the little details—the gleaming buttons, the perfectly tailored fit—that made her feel like a million bucks.

"Twins!" Laura exclaimed when Simran stepped out.

"Let's make it official," Simran said. "Shoes next, then accessories."

By the time they reached the checkout counter, their arms were full of bags. Laura glanced at Simran, hesitating.

"I can't get everything," she admitted. "Mum's already complaining about the electric bill this month."

Simran waved her off. "Don't worry about it. Aunt Dee gave me enough money to buy the whole store."

Laura's jaw dropped. "Your aunt is unreal. Who hands out two grand like that?"

"She does," Simran said with a shrug. "Don't argue. You're getting the shoes."

They left the shop grinning and made a beeline for Pizza Hut. The buffet was in full swing, with steaming trays of pizza, pasta, and garlic bread lining the counter.

"I'm going straight for the pepperoni," Laura declared, grabbing a plate.

Simran piled her plate high with veggie pizza and pasta bake. "I'm trying everything," she said, balancing a breadstick on top.

The girls ate until they could barely move, going back for seconds—and thirds—before finally collapsing into their booth with groans of satisfaction.

"This," Laura said, gesturing to the pile of empty plates, "is the life."

They spent the rest of the afternoon wandering through the

shops, picking up small trinkets and flipping through CDs at Our Price. Simran bought a shiny new Discman, while Laura finally found her coveted Tamagotchi.

By the time they boarded the bus home, their arms were heavy with shopping bags, and their feet were sore from hours of walking.

"I can't wait for the disco," Simran said, leaning her head against the window. "It's going to be epic."

Laura nodded, already daydreaming about Nick Patel.

Chapter 4: Family Ties

Back in Southall, Baljeet sat at her sewing machine, the steady hum filling the small dining room. A half-finished blouse destined for a Topshop display hung over the chair next to her. The sewing machine was a lifeline, a portal through which she turned bolts of fabric into money for her family. As she worked, her mind wandered to her eldest daughter.

"Simran must be on her way back by now," she thought, glancing at the clock on the wall. The thought of her daughter off shopping without a care in the world made Baljeet smile. But it also left a familiar pang of worry.

Simran was smart—brilliant, even. Her teachers often praised her creativity and quick wit. But the pressure of GCSEs was no joke, and Baljeet couldn't help but fret about whether Simran was truly ready.

"Maths," she muttered under her breath. "That one subject will be the death of her."

She thought back to her own childhood in Jalandhar, where education wasn't a choice for many girls. Baljeet had been

Friendship, Family and Fireworks

lucky. Her father, a progressive man for his time, had insisted she finish school before marrying. Still, her academic dreams had been cut short when her chachaji arranged her marriage to Rajinder, a young man from London.

Baljeet smiled at the memory of her first meeting with Rajinder. It had been awkward but sweet. He'd flown to India with his parents, and they'd met in her chacha's courtyard. Rajinder had been shy, barely meeting her gaze, but when their eyes did meet, there was a warmth she couldn't ignore.

The wedding had been a whirlwind—a week of loud dhol beats, colorful ceremonies, and endless trays of laddoos and jalebis. Baljeet's family had cried as they sent her off to London, their tears a mix of joy and sadness.

But life in London had been far from the dream she'd imagined. Baljeet's new mother-in-law, Dadi, had been a formidable woman with strong opinions about everything. Dadi made it clear that she favored her son and was skeptical of Baljeet's ability to handle the household.

"You're too modern," Dadi had once said, frowning at Baljeet's colorful salwar kameez.

But Baljeet had learned to navigate Dadi's moods. She'd worked tirelessly, cooking, cleaning, and caring for her family while never losing her smile. Over time, Dadi's sharp edges softened. Though she rarely admitted it aloud, Dadi often boasted to her friends at the gurdwara about how hardworking and respectful her daughter-in-law was.

Baljeet's thoughts were interrupted by the sound of Preeti and Amrit arguing in the next room.

"Stop pulling my hair!" Preeti shrieked.

"Mummy!" Amrit called. "She started it!"

"Bas karo!" Baljeet shouted, her voice carrying over the noise.

Chapter 4: Family Ties

"Preeti, help your brother with his spelling! Amrit, if you don't stop, no ice cream tonight!"

The room fell silent except for the faint sound of Manveer giggling.

Baljeet chuckled to herself, shaking her head. Managing four kids wasn't easy, but it was worth every headache. She thought about how Simran, at 15, had already taken on so much responsibility as the eldest. Simran was like a second mother to her siblings, helping with homework, breaking up fights, and even cooking dinner when Baljeet was too tired.

Still, Baljeet worried. "She's spending so much time with her friends," she thought. "What if she doesn't take her studies seriously? What if she struggles in her GCSEs?"

Baljeet's own mother had drilled into her the importance of hard work and resilience. She wanted the same for Simran, but it was hard to strike a balance between guiding her and letting her enjoy her teenage years.

She sighed and looked at the small stack of GCSE revision guides on the dining table. Simran had promised she'd study that evening after her shopping trip. Baljeet hoped she would stick to her word.

Just then, the front door creaked open. Simran's laughter echoed through the hallway as she and Laura stepped inside, bags rustling.

"Hi, Mum!" Simran called.

Baljeet peeked into the hallway, her heart warming at the sight of her daughter's flushed cheeks and sparkling eyes.

"Did you have fun?" she asked.

"The best!" Simran said, holding up one of her shopping bags. "We got the perfect outfits for the disco."

"And did you remember what I said about saving money?"

Friendship, Family and Fireworks

Baljeet raised an eyebrow.

Simran hesitated for half a second before grinning sheepishly. "We might have gone a little overboard…"

Baljeet shook her head, laughing. "As long as you don't forget to finish your homework later. Laura, beta, you're staying for dinner, right?"

Laura nodded shyly. "If that's okay, Aunty."

"Of course, it is. You're family," Baljeet said, ushering the girls into the kitchen.

As she served them steaming plates of rajma chawal, Baljeet felt a sense of peace settle over her. For all her worries, moments like this reminded her that everything would be okay. Simran was strong, resourceful, and kind.

Baljeet glanced at her daughter and thought, "She'll figure it out. She always does."

Chapter 5: Roots and Resilience

Baljeet leaned back in her chair after the girls had eaten and wandered upstairs. The quiet of the dining room, with only the faint hum of the refrigerator and the tick of the clock, gave her time to reflect. She often thought about how far her family had come and the sacrifices that had been made to build their life in Southall.

Her own childhood in Jalandhar was vivid in her mind, as though it had been only yesterday. Baljeet had been the youngest of three daughters in a family where sons were prized and daughters were seen as responsibilities. Her father, however, had been different.

"Padhai karo, Baljeet," he'd always said, pushing her to excel in school despite the whispers of disapproval from relatives. "A girl with an education can stand on her own two feet."

It was on a trip to Delhi with her father that her life had taken a significant turn. Her Chachaji, visiting from London, had mentioned a potential marriage match for Baljeet.

"She's smart, hardworking, and respectful," Chachaji had said.

Friendship, Family and Fireworks

"The boy is a good one—settled in London, with a family that values tradition."

Baljeet had felt a knot of anxiety tighten in her stomach. She wasn't ready to leave her family or her studies behind, but she knew saying no wasn't an option.

A few weeks later, she found herself on a flight to London, accompanied by her parents and Chachaji. It was her first time on an airplane, and though she was nervous, she couldn't help but marvel at the clouds outside the window.

On the same flight was a woman who would become one of Baljeet's closest friends—Gurpreet, Kiran's mother. Gurpreet had been traveling with her baby daughter, returning to her husband in London after visiting her family in Punjab.

The two women had struck up a conversation while waiting in the long immigration line at Heathrow. Baljeet, still overwhelmed by the whirlwind of her upcoming wedding, had found comfort in Gurpreet's calm demeanor and easy laughter.

"London is different, but you'll love it," Gurpreet had assured her. "Just keep your faith strong, and everything will fall into place."

Their friendship had only grown stronger over the years, with their families becoming as close as siblings. Simran and Kiran had grown up together, practically inseparable, and Gurpreet had become one of Baljeet's greatest sources of support during difficult times.

Dadi's Shadow

Life with Dadi, however, had been a different challenge. Baljeet's mother-in-law was a force of nature, with a sharp tongue and an unshakable belief in tradition. Dadi had made it clear

Chapter 5: Roots and Resilience

from the start that she didn't think Baljeet was good enough for her beloved Rajinder.

"You're too soft," Dadi had said on Baljeet's first day in the house. "You'll never be able to handle this family."

Baljeet had taken the criticism with a smile, choosing to focus on her new role as a wife and daughter-in-law. She'd spent hours in the kitchen, learning to cook Rajinder's favorite dishes, and had taken over the household chores without complaint.

Over time, Baljeet's quiet determination began to win Dadi over. Though she never admitted it directly, Dadi started boasting to her friends about her "hardworking bahu."

"She's always busy," Dadi would say at the gurdwara, her voice filled with a mix of pride and grudging admiration. "Even when she's tired, she never stops."

Rajinder's Journey

Rajinder, too, had his own story of resilience. As a young boy, he'd grown up in the shadow of the 1984 anti-Sikh riots in India. His parents had shielded him from much of the violence, but the fear and uncertainty of that time had left a mark on him.

When his parents passed away in a car accident a few years later, Rajinder was sent to live with his Baba and Dadi in Southall. Baba, a devout and wise man, had taken on the role of father figure, guiding Rajinder through his teenage years with patience and love.

It was Baba who had arranged Rajinder's marriage to Baljeet, trusting her to bring stability and joy to their home.

The Next Generation

Now, as Baljeet watched her own children grow, she felt a deep sense of responsibility. Simran, with her sharp mind and quick wit, reminded her so much of her younger self. But Baljeet worried that her daughter might not fully understand the value of hard work and sacrifice.

"Does she know how much we've given up for her to have this life?" Baljeet wondered.

She thought of her own mother, who had always reminded her to stay humble and grounded.

"Teach your children the value of gratitude," her mother had once said. "If they forget where they came from, they'll lose their way."

Baljeet sighed, glancing at the pile of laundry waiting to be folded. The weight of her family's history pressed on her shoulders, but it also filled her with pride.

Her daughter would find her way, just as she had.

Chapter 6: The Wisdom of Dadi

The next morning, the Gill household was bustling with activity. Baljeet was in the kitchen preparing aloo parathas for breakfast, while the children squabbled over the TV remote. In the midst of the chaos, Dadi emerged from her room, her dupatta neatly pinned, her wooden walking stick tapping softly against the tiled floor.

"Baljeet, I'm going to the gurdwara," Dadi announced, her tone commanding as always.

"Ji, Mataji," Baljeet replied, setting a steaming paratha on a plate. "I'll pack you some prashad for the ladies."

Dadi nodded approvingly and settled into her usual spot by the window while waiting. Though she was over seventy, Dadi carried herself with a dignity that made her seem almost regal. Her days revolved around her visits to the gurdwara, where she met her circle of friends—an exclusive group of formidable women who held court over chai and samosas after the morning prayers.

Friendship, Family and Fireworks

The Queen Bee of the Gurdwara

At the gurdwara, Dadi was in her element. She greeted her friends—Jeevan Kaur, Harjit Biji, and Sukhi Aunty—with a warm smile, but her presence demanded respect. The women gathered on the floor of the langar hall, their conversations a blend of religious discussions, gossip, and advice about family matters.

"Did you hear about Meena's granddaughter?" Harjit Biji began, sipping her chai. "She wants to become a doctor. Such a good girl."

"And what about your granddaughter, Avtar Kaur?" Sukhi Aunty asked, turning to Dadi.

Dadi's chest puffed with pride. "Simran is very clever. Top marks in her class. Always helping her mother and looking after her siblings."

"But she spends so much time with her friends," Jeevan Kaur added, her tone teasing. "You must keep an eye on her. Girls these days…"

Dadi smiled faintly but didn't respond. Inside, she was fiercely protective of Simran. Though she sometimes criticized her behind closed doors, Dadi would defend her family to anyone outside it.

After prayers, the women lingered for their usual banter, discussing everything from rising prices to the best remedies for joint pain. As they parted ways, Dadi felt a sense of satisfaction. These small moments of camaraderie gave her a sense of purpose and belonging.

Chapter 7: Rajinder's Balancing Act

While Dadi was at the gurdwara, Rajinder sat at the dining table, poring over the family's monthly expenses. A small business owner, he ran a modest corner shop that catered to the local community. It wasn't glamorous work, but it paid the bills and allowed him to provide for his family.

Rajinder often found himself caught between two worlds. On one hand, he wanted to preserve the traditions his parents and grandparents had instilled in him. On the other, he understood the importance of adapting to the modern world, especially for his children.

Simran was a perfect example of this delicate balance. She embraced her culture, helping with religious ceremonies and wearing salwar kameez to family events. But she was also fiercely independent, with dreams and ambitions that went beyond the boundaries of tradition.

"I don't want her to feel trapped," Rajinder thought, sipping his chai. "But I also don't want her to lose touch with who she is."

Friendship, Family and Fireworks

He glanced at a framed photo on the wall of his parents standing outside the Golden Temple in Amritsar. His father had been a stern but loving man who believed in discipline and hard work. Rajinder often wondered if he was too lenient with his own children.

His thoughts were interrupted by Simran bounding down the stairs, her hair still damp from the shower.

"Dad, can I borrow the car tonight for the disco?" she asked, her tone hopeful.

Rajinder raised an eyebrow. "Disco, huh? And how are those GCSE revision guides coming along?"

Simran hesitated, then grinned. "I promise I'll study all weekend. Please, Dad?"

Rajinder chuckled, shaking his head. "We'll see. But no late-night nonsense, okay?"

"Deal!" Simran said, giving him a quick hug before dashing back upstairs.

Rajinder watched her go, a mixture of pride and worry in his heart.

Chapter 8: Disco Preparations and Unbreakable Bonds

Simran's room buzzed with energy as her best friends gathered to prepare for the school disco. The air was filled with laughter, chatter, and the occasional clatter of a makeup brush falling to the floor. They weren't just getting ready; they were building up the excitement for a night they knew would be unforgettable.

Though they came from different backgrounds, the four of them were like pieces of a puzzle that fit perfectly together. Their friendship was built on love, respect, and an unspoken promise to always have each other's backs.

Simran: The Anchor

Simran was the glue that held the group together. As the eldest sibling in her family, she had a natural instinct to care for others. It showed in the way she always made sure everyone was included and heard. She was also fiercely loyal. If anyone dared mess with one of her friends, Simran would stand up for them without hesitation.

"Right," Simran said, smoothing down her black blazer as she checked herself in the mirror. "Let's get this straight—tonight, we're going to have fun, no drama, and no holding back. Got it?"

Her tone was playful, but the others knew she meant every word. Simran was their protector, their anchor.

Laura: The Dreamer

Laura sat cross-legged on Simran's bed, expertly applying eyeliner while listening to the chatter. Her pale blonde hair fell in soft waves around her face, and she was dressed in her Men in Black outfit, the sharp lines of her blazer contrasting with her usual casual style.

Laura's life at home was tough. Growing up in a chaotic council estate with four older sisters who had already left school and started their own families, she had learned early on to fend for herself. Yet, she never let her struggles dim her spirit.

"Do you think he'll notice me tonight?" Laura asked, biting her lip as she applied a touch of mascara.

"Nick Patel? Of course, he will!" Zara replied, throwing an arm around her.

"And if he doesn't, he's not worth it," Kiran added firmly.

Laura smiled, her heart swelling with gratitude. She knew she could always count on these girls to lift her up, even when she doubted herself.

Chapter 8: Disco Preparations and Unbreakable Bonds

Kiran: The Voice of Reason

Kiran, ever the practical one, was busy organizing the accessories strewn across Simran's desk. Her dark, curly hair framed her face as she held up different pairs of earrings for Zara to try.

Kiran came from a family steeped in tradition. Her mother and Simran's mother had been best friends since their youth, and their bond had extended to their daughters. Kiran was the sensible one of the group, often keeping the others grounded when their ideas got too wild.

"Simran, are you really going to wear those shoes?" Kiran teased, pointing at Simran's heeled loafers.

"What's wrong with them?" Simran shot back, pretending to be offended.

"Nothing," Kiran said with a grin. "But don't blame me when you're complaining about blisters halfway through the night."

The room erupted in laughter, and Simran tossed a pillow at Kiran, who caught it effortlessly.

Zara: The Firecracker

Zara was the life of the group, with a boldness that often led to both adventures and trouble. She had an infectious energy and a sharp wit that could disarm even the most serious of people.

"Forget the earrings—what we need is a strategy for the dance floor," Zara announced, striking a mock pose. "Who's going to lead the charge?"

"You, obviously," Simran replied with a laugh. "You'll probably drag half the school up to dance with you."

"Exactly," Zara said, throwing on a pair of oversized sunglasses to complete her look. "Because we don't do boring. That's not our style."

Their Bond

Though their personalities were wildly different, the girls had an unshakeable bond. Simran admired Laura's resilience, Laura found comfort in Kiran's steadiness, Kiran looked up to Simran's leadership, and they all relied on Zara's fearless spirit to keep things exciting.

They also shared an unspoken understanding of each other's struggles. Laura often marveled at how Kiran and Simran's mothers cared for her, offering her food, clothes, and advice when her own family couldn't. Kiran admired Zara's courage to speak her mind, something she wished she could do more often. Simran cherished how her friends made her life richer and more colorful.

"You know," Laura said suddenly, her voice softer now, "I don't know what I'd do without you girls."

"Don't get mushy on us now," Zara teased, but her grin softened the words.

Simran stepped forward, placing a hand on Laura's shoulder. "You'll never have to. No matter what happens, we've got you."

The others nodded in agreement, the room falling silent for a moment as the weight of their bond settled over them.

The Final Touches

As the clock ticked closer to disco time, the girls finished their preparations. Lip gloss was applied, earrings chosen, and shoes double-checked. Simran grabbed her black clutch bag and gave

Chapter 8: Disco Preparations and Unbreakable Bonds

one final look in the mirror.

"Alright," she said, turning to her friends. "We look amazing. Let's go and show everyone what we're made of."

They grabbed their coats and headed downstairs, their laughter echoing through the house. Baljeet, watching them from the kitchen, smiled to herself. She could see how much these girls meant to each other and felt a deep sense of gratitude that her daughter had found such a supportive group of friends.

The night was just beginning, and they were ready to take it on—together.

Chapter 9: The Night Comes Alive

The cold November air nipped at the girls as they stepped out of Simran's house and made their way to the school disco. The streetlights bathed the sidewalks in a soft orange glow, and their laughter filled the quiet suburban streets of Southall.

"I'm calling it now," Zara declared, pointing dramatically at Laura. "Nick Patel is going to be speechless when he sees you."

"Let's not jinx it," Laura replied, her cheeks tinged pink.

"Don't worry, Laura," Simran said, looping an arm around her best friend. "You look amazing. He'd be a fool not to notice."

Kiran smiled, walking a step behind the others. "I just hope the DJ knows what he's doing tonight. Last time, all we got was Spice Girls and Aqua on repeat."

"I like *Barbie Girl!*" Zara exclaimed, earning groans from the rest of the group.

Chapter 9: The Night Comes Alive

The Disco Scene

The school hall had been transformed into a makeshift nightclub. Twinkling fairy lights lined the walls, a disco ball cast shimmering patterns across the room, and the booming bass of R&B hits filled the air. Tables along the sides were piled high with party food—crisps, samosas, mini sausages, and cupcakes—while a drinks station offered fizzy drinks in every flavor.

The girls stepped inside, their confidence soaring as heads turned to admire their coordinated Men in Black outfits. The sharp pinstriped blazers and trousers were a bold choice, but they pulled it off effortlessly.

"Right," Zara announced, scanning the room. "Time to make an entrance."

Simran chuckled and nudged her forward. "Go on then, Miss Firecracker. Lead the way."

They moved together, a synchronized force of fun and charisma. The DJ transitioned into *No Diggity* by Blackstreet, and the girls cheered, heading straight for the dance floor.

Nick Patel

Laura's eyes flitted nervously across the room until they landed on Nick Patel, standing near the drinks table with his friends. Dressed in a sharp shirt and jeans, he exuded a relaxed charm that made him one of the most popular boys in school.

"Alright, Laura," Simran whispered. "This is your chance. Go say hi."

"What? No! I can't just walk up to him," Laura hissed back.

"Don't worry," Zara said, grinning mischievously. "I've got this."

Friendship, Family and Fireworks

Before Laura could protest, Zara waved in Nick's direction. "Oi, Nick! Over here!"

Nick turned, his face lighting up as he saw the group. He strolled over, his easy confidence making Laura's stomach flip.

"Hey, Simran. Zara. Kiran. Laura," he said, nodding at each of them. His eyes lingered on Simran a moment longer, and she noticed his smile widen.

"Looking sharp, ladies," Nick added, gesturing to their outfits.

"Thanks," Simran replied, her tone warm but casual. "We thought we'd change it up a bit. You're looking good too."

"Yeah, not bad," Zara chimed in, earning a laugh from everyone, including Nick.

Laura stood frozen, her nerves getting the better of her. Simran, noticing her hesitation, decided to step in.

"So, Nick," Simran said, leaning in slightly. "Did you know Laura's a huge fan of *Men in Black*? She practically made us dress like this."

Laura shot Simran a panicked look, but Nick's grin softened the moment.

"Really? That's cool," Nick said, turning to Laura. "I've got to admit, you all nailed it. Especially you."

Laura's cheeks turned bright red, but she managed a shy smile. "Thanks."

The Dance Floor and Teachers Letting Loose

As the DJ transitioned into *Return of the Mack* by Mark Morrison, the girls couldn't resist any longer. They dragged Nick onto the dance floor, where a growing crowd of students was already swaying to the beat.

The usually strict teachers surprised everyone by joining in,

Chapter 9: The Night Comes Alive

their stiff demeanors melting away as they danced awkwardly but enthusiastically in the corner.

"Miss Evans has got moves!" Zara exclaimed, pointing at the English teacher who was twirling under the disco ball.

"Not bad for someone who usually tells us to sit down and shut up," Kiran added, laughing.

The music shifted again, this time to *Rhythm of the Night* by Corona, and the energy in the room skyrocketed. The girls threw themselves into the music, their inhibitions gone as they danced in sync with the crowd. Even Laura, who had started the night so shy, was laughing and spinning, her confidence bolstered by Nick's attention.

A Moment of Truth

After several songs, Simran noticed Nick lingering near her again. He was easy to talk to, and they quickly fell into a rhythm of teasing and joking. But Simran couldn't ignore the way Laura kept glancing over, her expression a mix of longing and worry.

"You're funny," Nick said, leaning closer to Simran as the music thumped around them.

"Thanks," Simran replied, her tone light but firm. "But you know, Nick, Laura's the real star here. She's got great taste in movies and… other things."

Nick blinked, then glanced at Laura, who was nervously sipping her drink by the food table. A flicker of understanding crossed his face.

"Laura's great," he said, nodding slowly.

"She really is," Simran said, giving him a meaningful look. "You should tell her that."

Nick hesitated for a moment, then smiled. "Yeah, I think I

will."

The Night Ends on a High Note

By the end of the night, Laura was glowing. Nick had asked her to dance, and though it was just one song, it felt like a dream come true. The girls regrouped near the food table, munching on cupcakes and laughing about the night's events.

"I can't believe you did that," Laura said, turning to Simran. "You set me up with him."

"Of course, I did," Simran replied, grinning. "What are friends for?"

As the disco wound down and the lights came up, the girls linked arms and made their way out into the chilly night. Their chatter and laughter echoed through the streets as they walked back to Simran's house, where Baljeet had left snacks waiting for them.

The night wasn't over yet. They stayed up until 4 a.m., reliving every moment of the disco, from the teachers' antics to Laura's dance with Nick. As the first light of dawn crept through the curtains, Simran looked around at her friends, her heart full.

No matter where life took them, she knew they'd always have each other.

Chapter 10: Morning Reflections and Family Threads

The faint rays of dawn filtered through Simran's bedroom window as the four friends lay sprawled across her room, surrounded by empty crisp packets, half-eaten samosas, and discarded blankets. The laughter and excitement of the night before lingered in the air, but a peaceful quiet had settled over them.

"Did we really stay up till 4 a.m.?" Kiran mumbled, her voice thick with sleep as she hugged a pillow.

"We did," Simran said, stifling a yawn. "Totally worth it, though."

Laura, lying on her back with her arms folded behind her head, smiled. "Best night ever. Thanks, Simran. You didn't have to, but you always make everything better."

Simran waved her off. "Stop being so soppy. You would've done the same for me."

Friendship, Family and Fireworks

A Family Moment

Downstairs, the smell of freshly made parathas wafted through the house. Baljeet was up early, as usual, preparing breakfast for the family. As she worked, her thoughts drifted to Simran.

Simran was a bright, hardworking girl, but the stress of GCSEs was looming large. Baljeet worried if her daughter was juggling too much—school, friends, and family responsibilities. She wiped her hands on her apron, her gaze softening as she thought about how much Simran had grown.

"Morning, Mum," Simran said, appearing in the kitchen doorway, her hair tied up in a messy bun.

"Morning, beta," Baljeet replied, smiling warmly. "Did you have fun last night?"

"It was amazing. Thanks for letting the girls stay over." Simran grabbed a piece of toast and leaned against the counter.

Baljeet raised an eyebrow, her lips twitching into a knowing smile. "So… was it worth bunking school to go shopping?"

Simran froze mid-bite, her eyes wide. "Wait—what? How did you know?"

Baljeet laughed softly, her tone teasing but kind. "I'm your mother. I know everything. And don't worry, your dad won't say anything either. He told me it's your little secret, but next time, just tell me, okay?"

Simran exhaled in relief, her cheeks turning pink. "I promise."

Baljeet nodded, her expression turning serious. "I trust you, Simran. I know you'll make good choices, but I also want you to focus on your studies. Your GCSEs are important."

"I know, Mum," Simran said, her voice steady. "I won't let you down."

Chapter 10: Morning Reflections and Family Threads

Dadi's Social Life at the Gurdwara

Upstairs, Dadi was preparing for her weekly trip to the gurdwara. She sat in front of her dressing table, carefully pinning her dupatta in place. Despite her stern demeanor at home, the gurdwara was where she came alive.

"Simran!" Dadi called out.

Simran appeared at the door. "Yes, Dadi?"

"Beta, help me with my shawl. I can't go to the gurdwara looking like a mess."

Simran smiled and stepped forward, wrapping the shawl neatly around Dadi's shoulders. "There you go. You look perfect."

"Haan, bas thik hai," Dadi muttered, but her eyes twinkled with gratitude.

At the gurdwara, Dadi was a queen among her friends. She spent hours chatting, exchanging stories, and laughing in the company of women who shared her memories of Punjab. Though she rarely expressed it at home, she often bragged to her friends about Baljeet's dedication to the family.

"My bahu is hardworking, no doubt," Dadi would say, sipping chai with her friends. "She never complains, no matter how much work there is."

"Then why are you always scolding her?" one of her friends teased.

Dadi waved her hand dismissively. "It's my job to keep her on her toes. But between us, she's the best bahu I could have asked for."

Friendship, Family and Fireworks

Rajinder's Balancing Act

Meanwhile, Rajinder was busy tinkering with the family's VW Golf in the driveway. The car was Simran's favorite, and she often joked that she'd inherit it when she turned 18.

As he worked, his mind wandered to his own struggles of balancing tradition and modernity. He wanted his children to stay connected to their roots, but he also recognized their desire for independence.

"Papa," Simran said, stepping outside with a cup of tea.

"Haan, beta," Rajinder replied, taking the cup and setting it on the car's hood.

"Thanks for not ratting me out to Mum," Simran said with a sheepish grin.

Rajinder chuckled. "You're growing up, Simran. I want you to enjoy these years, but don't forget who you are and where you come from."

Simran nodded, her heart swelling with appreciation. "I won't, Papa. I promise."

Preparations for the Disco Aftermath

Back inside, the girls were slowly waking up, their grogginess fading as the smell of parathas drew them to the kitchen. They recapped every detail of the disco, from Laura's dance with Nick to the teachers' hilarious attempts at dancing.

"What's the plan for today?" Zara asked, munching on a piece of toast.

"First, breakfast," Simran said. "Then, maybe we help my mum with some sewing. She's got a big order for Topshop, and we could make it fun."

Chapter 10: Morning Reflections and Family Threads

"Sounds good," Kiran said. "And maybe we can listen to the CDs we bought at Our Price."

Laura smiled, leaning back in her chair. "Honestly, I'd rather be here with you guys than anywhere else."

Baljeet, overhearing from the stove, turned and smiled at the girls. "You're always welcome here, Laura. All of you are."

The warmth in the room was palpable, a testament to the unbreakable bonds of friendship and family that tied them all together.

Chapter 11: The Calm Before the Storm

The days following the disco brought a sense of normalcy back to Simran's life. School resumed its usual rhythm, with GCSE mock exams looming like a storm cloud on the horizon. Teachers buzzed about revision schedules and exam techniques, and the pressure in the classroom was palpable.

Simran sat at her desk in English, absently twirling her pen as she stared at the essay prompt on the board. Laura, seated next to her, leaned over and whispered, "You okay?"

"Yeah," Simran replied, though her furrowed brow said otherwise.

Laura gave her a knowing look. "You'll be fine. You're like the smartest person I know."

Simran smiled faintly. "Thanks, but sometimes it feels like there's so much riding on this. Mum's always saying how important it is, and I don't want to let her down."

Chapter 11: The Calm Before the Storm

Baljeet's Worries

Back at home, Baljeet was stitching a hem on a deep blue dress bound for Topshop's winter collection. Her hands moved expertly, but her thoughts were far away.

"How's Simran doing with her studies?" she asked Rajinder, who was seated nearby, sipping his tea.

"She's doing well," Rajinder replied. "She's a smart girl, just like you."

Baljeet sighed. "I know she is, but GCSEs are so important. I want her to have opportunities we never had. What if it's too much for her?"

Rajinder set his cup down and gave her a reassuring smile. "Simran is capable of more than you think. She has your determination and my... charm."

Baljeet rolled her eyes, but his words eased her worries.

A Moment with Dadi

That evening, Simran found herself in the living room with Dadi, who was watching an old Bollywood movie on TV. Simran sat down beside her, and Dadi glanced over, her sharp eyes softening.

"Beta, why the long face?"

"Just school stuff," Simran admitted.

Dadi patted her hand. "Don't let it get to you. You're a Gill. We're made of strong stuff. You'll make us proud."

Simran smiled, her heart lifting at Dadi's unexpected encouragement.

Friendship, Family and Fireworks

The Friends' Pact

The next day during lunch, Simran, Laura, Kiran, and Zara gathered at their usual spot under the big oak tree in the schoolyard. The November chill had them wrapped in scarves and coats, but their spirits were high.

"Alright," Zara said, leaning forward with a determined look. "We need a plan to survive these GCSEs without losing our minds."

Kiran nodded. "Study sessions at each other's houses. We'll take turns, and whoever hosts has to provide snacks."

"I'm in," Laura said. "And if anyone tries to back out, we'll drag them kicking and screaming."

Simran laughed. "Deal. But no distractions, Zara. Last time, you spent the whole time drawing hearts in your notebook."

"What can I say?" Zara replied with a grin. "I'm a romantic."

They all laughed, their sisterhood bond is all they need against the mounting stress of exams.

An Unexpected Visit

One evening, as Simran was in her room revising, there was a knock on her door.

"Come in," she called.

Baljeet entered, holding a tray with two cups of chai. "Thought you could use a break."

Simran set her textbook aside and smiled. "Thanks, Mum."

Baljeet sat on the edge of the bed, handing her a cup. "I know I push you sometimes, but it's only because I want the best for you."

"I know," Simran said softly.

Chapter 11: The Calm Before the Storm

"You're doing great, beta. Just remember, no matter what happens, we're proud of you."

Simran's throat tightened with emotion. "Thanks, Mum. That means a lot."

A New Focus

With her family's support and her friends by her side, Simran felt a renewed sense of determination. She threw herself into her studies, balancing revision sessions with moments of laughter and fun with Laura, Kiran, and Zara.

The four of them tackled their GCSE preparation as a team, holding each other accountable and celebrating small victories along the way. Kiran's house became their favorite study spot, thanks to her mum's endless supply of pakoras and chai.

Even Laura, who often struggled with school, found herself improving. "I think you lot are rubbing off on me," she joked one evening as she successfully solved a tricky math problem.

"That's what friends are for," Simran said, her eyes shining with pride.

Moving Forward

As the weeks flew by, the bond between the girls only grew stronger. They celebrated Zara's birthday with a spontaneous karaoke session, helped Laura write an essay she'd been dreading, and cheered when Kiran aced her science quiz.

Simran's family also noticed her growing confidence. Dadi bragged about her to her friends at the gurdwara, while Rajinder started calling her "Professor Gill" around the house.

One evening, as Simran was packing her school bag for the

next day, she paused and smiled. Life wasn't perfect, but with her family's love and her friends' unwavering support, she felt ready to face whatever came next.

Chapter 12: Shadows of Crisis

The warmth of winter began to fade as a sudden chill of worry swept through the Gill household. It started with a phone call one rainy evening. Rajinder answered, and his face immediately grew tense. His words were short and urgent.

"Hanji, chachaji... what happened? Okay, okay, we'll come tomorrow. Don't worry."

Baljeet entered the room, drying her hands on her dupatta. "What's wrong?"

Rajinder's expression was grave. "It's Chachaji. He's been unwell, and now they're saying he might need surgery. We'll need to go to Birmingham for a few days."

Baljeet's face fell. Chachaji was like a second father to Rajinder, and the thought of him suffering filled her with unease.

Simran overheard from the staircase. "Papa? Is everything okay?"

Rajinder nodded quickly. "It's nothing for you to worry about, beta. We'll handle it."

But Simran couldn't shake the feeling that the family was on the brink of something heavy.

A Secret Shared

The next day at school, Simran found herself distracted, her mind replaying her father's worried tone. Laura nudged her during lunch. "What's up? You've been quiet all day."

Simran hesitated but decided to share. "It's my Chachaji. He's really unwell, and I think my parents are worried it's serious."

Kiran immediately put her hand on Simran's shoulder. "I'm so sorry, Simran. Is there anything we can do to help?"

Zara chimed in. "Yeah, seriously. If you need anything, just let us know."

Laura leaned closer, her voice soft. "And don't forget, you're not alone. We're here for you, okay?"

Simran felt a lump rise in her throat. She looked around at her friends, their faces full of concern, and nodded. "Thanks, guys. That really means a lot."

Nick's Confession

Later that afternoon, as Simran was gathering her books from her locker, Nick Patel approached her, looking uncharacteristically nervous.

"Hey, Simran," he said, shoving his hands into his pockets.
"Hey, Nick. What's up?"
"Can we talk for a second? It's… kind of important."
Simran tilted her head, intrigued. "Sure."
They stepped into the quiet of the empty music room. Nick hesitated, running a hand through his hair. "Look, I wanted to

Chapter 12: Shadows of Crisis

say thanks for what you did at the disco. You didn't have to, but you made things a lot easier for me and Laura."

Simran smiled. "No problem. You two make a cute couple."

Nick's face clouded. "That's the thing... I really like Laura. Like, *really* like her. But my family..." He trailed off, his voice heavy with frustration.

"They wouldn't approve because she's not Hindu," Simran guessed.

Nick nodded. "My parents are... traditional. They've always said I should marry someone from our community. And Laura's amazing, but I don't know how to make them see that."

Simran folded her arms, considering his words. "Does Laura know how you feel?"

"No," Nick admitted, looking down. "I haven't told her. I didn't want to hurt her, but I don't want to keep her in the dark either."

Simran's heart ached for her best friend. Laura had always dreamed of a love story that would make her feel special, and now that it was within reach, it came with complications.

"Nick," Simran said gently, "if you care about Laura, you owe it to her to be honest. But you also need to be honest with your family. They might surprise you."

Nick nodded slowly, his expression thoughtful. "You're right. I'll talk to her first. Thanks, Simran. You're a good friend."

The Strength of Friendship

That evening, Simran told the girls about Nick's confession during their usual phone catch-up.

"I knew it!" Zara exclaimed. "I knew he was head over heels for her."

Friendship, Family and Fireworks

"But what about his family?" Laura asked, her voice tinged with worry.

"Nick's going to talk to them," Simran assured her. "But he wants to be honest with you first. He really does care about you, Laura."

Laura's eyes filled with tears. "I don't know what to say. I've always wanted this, but not if it's going to hurt him or his family."

Kiran spoke up, her tone firm. "Laura, you deserve to be happy. If Nick's willing to fight for you, then you should give him a chance. And if his family needs convincing, we'll help. That's what friends are for."

Zara nodded. "Exactly. We've got your back, Laura."

Simran smiled, her heart swelling with pride. These girls weren't just her friends—they were her sisters.

A Family Departure

Two days later, the Gills packed their VW Golf and headed to Birmingham to see Chachaji. The drive was long and quiet, with only the occasional comment from Dadi about how cold it was. Simran sat in the back, staring out the window, her mind swirling with thoughts of her family and her friends.

When they arrived, they were greeted by worried faces and hurried hugs. Chachaji was frail but still smiled when he saw them.

"Rajinder, Baljeet," he said weakly, "you didn't have to come all this way."

"Of course we did, Chachaji," Rajinder said, his voice thick with emotion. "You're family."

Simran watched as her father and uncle exchanged a heartfelt embrace, and she felt a renewed sense of gratitude for the bonds

Chapter 12: Shadows of Crisis

that held her family together.

Laura and Nick's Conversation

While Simran was away, Nick finally mustered the courage to talk to Laura. They met at the local park, the crisp winter air adding a blush to Laura's cheeks.
"Hey," Nick said, his voice nervous.
"Hey," Laura replied, her heart pounding.
Nick took a deep breath. "I like you, Laura. I have for a long time. But there's something I need to tell you."
He explained his family's expectations and his fears about their disapproval. Laura listened quietly, her eyes shimmering with unshed tears.
"I don't want to lose you," Nick said finally. "But I don't know how to make this work."
Laura reached out and took his hand. "We'll figure it out together. I don't care what anyone else thinks. I care about you."

A New Challenge

When Simran returned from Birmingham, she was greeted with hugs from her friends and the news about Laura and Nick's conversation.
"Looks like we have some work to do," Simran said with a grin.
"What do you mean?" Laura asked.
"Convincing Nick's family that you're perfect for him," Simran replied.
The four friends exchanged determined looks. They'd faced

challenges before, but nothing could stand in the way of their love and loyalty for one another.

Chapter 13: Facing Traditions

The following week, Nick decided it was time to tell his parents about Laura. Simran, Laura, Kiran, and Zara were on edge as they waited for updates. Laura was the most nervous, pacing back and forth in Simran's room while the others tried to calm her.

"What if they hate me?" Laura asked, her voice trembling.

"They won't hate you," Kiran said firmly. "And if they do, that's their problem, not yours."

"But what if Nick caves under the pressure?" Laura's voice dropped to a whisper. "What if he decides I'm not worth it?"

Simran placed her hands on Laura's shoulders. "Stop. Nick cares about you, and he's willing to stand up to his family for you. That says everything. You just have to trust him—and yourself."

Laura nodded, her eyes brimming with gratitude. "Thanks, guys. I don't know what I'd do without you."

"Probably stress-eat an entire pizza," Zara teased, lightening the mood.

Friendship, Family and Fireworks

They all laughed, and for a moment, the tension eased.

Nick's Family Dinner

At Nick's house, the atmosphere was far from light. He sat at the dining table with his parents, the rich aroma of daal and rotis wafting from the kitchen. His father, Arun Patel, was reading the newspaper, while his mother, Meena, set down a plate of pickles.

"I need to tell you something," Nick began, his voice steady despite the nerves bubbling inside him.

Both parents looked up, curious but not alarmed.

"There's someone I like," he continued. "Her name is Laura."

Meena's expression shifted to one of mild concern. "Laura? That's not a Hindu name."

"No, she's not Hindu," Nick admitted. "But she's kind, smart, and respectful. I really care about her."

Arun put down his paper, his brow furrowing. "Nick, we've always taught you the importance of our culture and traditions. Marrying someone outside of that… it complicates things."

"I understand," Nick said, "but I want you to meet her before you decide. She deserves a chance."

Meena exchanged a look with Arun. "We'll think about it," she said finally.

Nick left the table feeling both relieved and apprehensive. The hardest part was over, but the battle was far from won.

Chapter 13: Facing Traditions

The Plan

When Nick shared the news with Laura and the group, they immediately sprang into action.

"Okay," Zara said, "we need to show them the Laura we know. Sweet, kind, and completely lovable."

Laura blushed. "You're making me sound like a golden retriever."

Kiran laughed. "Basically, yes. But seriously, this is about making them see the real you."

Simran nodded. "We'll help. Let's figure out what makes them tick. Nick, what do your parents value most?"

"Family, tradition, and respect," Nick said. "They're big on keeping up appearances, too."

"Then we'll show them Laura's got all of that," Simran said confidently.

The Meeting

The following Saturday, Nick invited Laura over to meet his parents. Simran, Kiran, and Zara helped Laura prepare, picking out a modest yet elegant outfit—a soft blue salwar kameez borrowed from Kiran's wardrobe.

"You look amazing," Simran said as they gave Laura a final once-over. "Nick's parents won't know what hit them."

Laura smiled nervously. "Thanks, guys. Wish me luck."

At Nick's house, Meena greeted Laura with a polite but reserved smile. Arun's expression was harder to read, but he didn't seem outright hostile.

"Thank you for inviting me," Laura said, her tone respectful.

Meena nodded. "It's nice to meet you, Laura. Nick's told us a lot about you."

Over dinner, Laura made an effort to connect with them. She complimented Meena's cooking, asked Arun about his work, and shared stories about her own family. Though she avoided mentioning the darker aspects of her upbringing, she spoke warmly about how Simran's family had welcomed her into their home.

By the end of the evening, Meena's demeanor had softened. "You're very polite, Laura," she said. "It's clear you've been raised to respect others."

"Thank you," Laura replied, her heart swelling with hope.

Support from the Friends

Back at Simran's house that evening, the girls waited anxiously for Laura to return and tell them how it went. When she finally arrived, her face was a mixture of relief and exhaustion.

"Well?" Zara asked, practically bouncing with anticipation.

"They didn't hate me," Laura said, collapsing onto Simran's bed. "Meena was actually… nice. Arun was harder to read, but he didn't seem angry."

"That's a win," Kiran said. "What happens next?"

"Nick said his parents want to think about it," Laura replied. "So I guess we wait."

"Whatever happens, we're here for you," Simran said firmly.

Laura smiled. "I know. You guys are the best."

Chapter 13: Facing Traditions

A Sudden Emergency

Just as things seemed to be settling down, a new crisis emerged. Rajinder received a call from his cousin in India, delivering devastating news: his Babaji had passed away.

The family was heartbroken, especially Dadi, who had been close to her late husband. Plans were quickly made for Rajinder and Dadi to travel to India for the funeral.

Baljeet, overwhelmed with the logistics, leaned heavily on Simran. "Beta, I need you to help with the younger ones while your dad is away," she said. "I can't do this alone."

"Of course, Mum," Simran said, her voice steady despite the weight of responsibility settling on her shoulders.

Strength in Unity

As the family prepared for Rajinder and Dadi's departure, Simran leaned on her friends for support. They helped her manage her siblings, keep up with schoolwork, and stay strong for her mum.

"You've got this," Laura said one evening as they sat in Simran's room. "If anyone can handle all this, it's you."

Simran smiled, grateful beyond words for her friends.

Nick's Parents Decide

A week later, Nick's parents invited Laura over again. This time, Simran went along for moral support, sitting quietly in the background while Laura spoke to Meena and Arun.

"We've talked a lot about this," Meena said, her tone serious. "And while it's not what we envisioned for Nick, we can see how much he cares about you. That's what matters most."

Laura's eyes filled with tears. "Thank you. I promise I'll never let you down."

As they left, Nick pulled Simran aside. "Thanks for everything, Simran. I couldn't have done this without you."

"You're welcome," she said, smiling. "Now go make her happy."

Moving Forward

With Nick's parents' blessing and the Gills slowly adjusting to their loss, life began to find its rhythm again. The friends grew closer than ever, their bond forged in the fires of love and loss.

Simran, ever the anchor of the group, felt a renewed sense of purpose. Whatever challenges lay ahead, she knew she could face them with her family and friends by her side.

Chapter 14: A Celebration to Remember

The buzz of excitement filled the Gill household as preparations were underway for a grand Lohri celebration. The festival, traditionally marking the end of winter, felt especially symbolic this year. After weeks of emotional ups and downs—Rajinder's loss, Nick's family drama, and the everyday hustle of life—this was a chance to celebrate love, resilience, and togetherness.

The house smelled of freshly made gur (jaggery), popcorn, and gajak. Baljeet had worked tirelessly to make the occasion perfect, enlisting Simran to help with decorations. Dadi, despite her recent sorrow, had insisted on hosting this gathering.

"We need to honor Babaji," Dadi said firmly. "He loved seeing the family together."

Friendship, Family and Fireworks

The Guests Arrive

As the evening approached, guests began arriving, filling the Gill home with chatter and laughter. Nick and Laura walked in together, hand in hand, earning a knowing look from Simran. Kiran and Zara soon followed, their smiles wide as they greeted everyone.

Simran, dressed in a vibrant pink salwar kameez with gold detailing, was the picture of grace as she flitted between guests, making sure everyone felt welcome.

"You've outdone yourself," Laura whispered, pulling Simran aside.

"Anything for family," Simran said with a wink.

Dancing Around the Bonfire

As night fell, everyone gathered in the backyard, where a large bonfire crackled and roared. The warmth of the flames lit up the faces of those who danced around it, hands clapping to the beat of traditional Punjabi dhols.

Nick, despite his awkward first attempts, joined the bhangra line, earning cheers and laughs. Laura stood to the side, laughing uncontrollably as Simran demonstrated the moves to him.

"You're terrible at this," Simran teased.

"Hey, I'm trying!" Nick said, grinning.

The four friends found themselves dancing together, the flames casting long shadows as they laughed and twirled.

Chapter 14: A Celebration to Remember

A Quiet Moment

Later in the evening, as the festivities slowed, Simran sat beside Dadi, watching the younger children roast peanuts and toss sesame seeds into the fire.

"You've grown so much, beta," Dadi said softly. "Babaji would have been proud."

Simran looked at her grandmother, surprised by the rare words of praise. "Thank you, Dadi."

Dadi patted her hand. "Your mother deserves much of the credit. She's a remarkable woman, even if I don't say it often enough."

Simran smiled, her heart swelling with pride. "She learned from you."

A Toast to Friendship

Inside, the four friends gathered around the dining table, plates piled high with samosas, pakoras, and gulab jamuns.

"To us," Zara said, raising her glass of mango juice.

"To never giving up," Kiran added.

"To being each other's family," Laura said, her voice catching slightly.

Simran raised her glass last. "And to a future where we keep dancing, laughing, and showing the world what we're made of."

They clinked their glasses together, their bond unshaken by the trials they had faced.

Looking Ahead

As the evening wound down and the last of the guests departed, the four friends stayed back, sprawled across the floor of Simran's room.

"Can you believe how much has happened?" Laura said, staring at the ceiling.

"I know," Kiran replied. "It feels like we've lived a whole lifetime in just a few weeks."

Simran smiled. "And through it all, we've had each other."

Zara sat up, her eyes sparkling. "Let's make a pact. No matter what happens, we stay like this—always together, always looking out for each other."

They all placed their hands in the center, sealing the promise with a shared laugh.

The Final Scene

The night ended with Simran stepping out onto the balcony, the crisp air brushing her cheeks. She looked up at the stars, feeling a deep sense of gratitude.

Her family, though imperfect, was her anchor. Her friends, though different, were her strength. And her future, though uncertain, was hers to shape.

"Whatever happens," she whispered, "I'm ready."

And with that, Simran stepped back inside, closing the chapter on one unforgettable season of her life and opening the door to endless possibilities ahead.

Printed in Dunstable, United Kingdom